The Seven Voyages of Sinbad the Sailor

Retold by

SAID

Illustrated by

Rashin

Translated by

David Henry Wilson

North South

Sinbad—a Hero from the *Thousand and One Nights*

The tale of "Sinbad the Sailor" is part of the rich collection of stories that make up the *Thousand and One Nights*. The stories are all told within a framing subplot that is shaped by the ingenious narrator Scheherazade.

Scheherazade is the daughter of the vizier, and she is determined to outwit the vengeful, wife-killing king. The only weapon this beautiful, well-read young woman has is good stories, and so she cleverly tells him an exciting story every night but keeps him in suspense by not revealing the ending until the next day. By this trick she survives for 1,001 nights. In the end, not only is her life spared, but the king makes her his queen.

The roots of the *Thousand and One Nights* go back more than two thousand years. There is no known author or first edition. The contents changed through the centuries, with new tales being added and others rewritten or discarded. The story of Sinbad the Sailor only became part of the collection in Antoine Galland's French version, published in 1704.

Galland's twelve-volume edition was the start of an enthusiastic reception of Oriental tales throughout Europe, and even today the stories from the *Thousand and One Nights* are still regarded as one of the most beautiful gifts that the East has offered to the world.

The fantastic story of the merchant Sinbad has lost none of its charm. Sinbad is a veritable powerhouse. His responses are always human, both in his despair and in his good nature. His adventures have never broken his spirit or left him embittered, but on the contrary have made him wiser. He is happy to return to his hometown and to enjoy a life of quiet contentment there. The following wise words were written by the Persian poet Rumi, but they might just as easily have come from Sinbad himself:

"Even though you may be led astray by the world, there is a treasure hidden deep within you. Open your inner eye, and return at last to where you came from."

CONTENTS

Sinbad the Sailor

During the reign of Harun al Rashid, Caliph of Baghdad, there lived two men called Sinbad; one was a sailor and the other a porter. The latter had great difficulty earning enough to feed his family, whereas the former had so much gold and silver that he did not know where to put it all. He had slaves and lived in a palace. The walls were covered with paintings and decorations, the rooms were sprinkled with rosewater, and perfumes mingled with scents from the flowers that grew in the gardens all around.

One day a man came to Sinbad the Porter and said, "Will you carry this load for me to a certain place?"

Sinbad was pleased and agreed to carry the load. The stranger gave him the fee, told him the address, and left. The route led past the house of Sinbad the Sailor. In front of the house, the grounds had been swept and watered, and the place was cool and shady. As the porter was tired, he laid down his burden in order to take a rest.

From inside the house he heard the singing of birds, music, and the voices of young people. He looked in and saw servants and slaves, and his nose was filled with the scent of fine food. Then he raised his eyes to heaven and said, "Almighty God! No mortal man can object to whatever you do. No one may ask you why you act in this manner and in no other. Some lead peaceful lives, and others lead lives of suffering. While some enjoy the shade of happiness, I live in the daily heat of misery. And yet the others are like me, and I am like them."

Scarcely had he spoken these words when a fine gentleman came through the doorway and said, "Sir, the owner of this house would like to speak with you."

The porter hesitated at first, but then he picked up his load, laid it down in the vestibule of the house, and followed the man into a great hall. There he saw an assembly of people seated in a wide circle around the owner. When the porter entered, he gave his greetings, kissed the floor, and thought, Only in paradise could there be such a place. The people returned his greetings and bade him welcome. The owner, however, gave him special greetings, invited him to sit by his side, and asked him his name and his profession.

"Sire! My name is Sinbad the Porter, and I am a poor man."

The owner said to him, "Once more, you are welcome, porter. You should know that I too am called Sinbad: Sinbad the Sailor."

Then he sent for some food to give to his guest. Only after the porter had eaten did the owner speak again. "I would like you now to repeat the words that you uttered earlier."

On hearing this the porter lowered his head and said, "By God, sire, do not be offended by those words. Weariness and the sufferings of poverty often lead men to say stupid things."

"Do not think," replied the owner, "that I am angry with you. I regard you as my brother, and you have nothing to fear."

When the porter had repeated the words he had spoken, the owner said, "Now I shall tell you the story of how I came to own this house and so much wealth. Because it was only after heavy losses, many obstacles, and endless sufferings that I achieved such prosperity. I made seven voyages, and each one forms a wondrous tale that should be written in gold to serve as an example to all."

He then began his tale as follows: "My father, who was a rich merchant, died when I was a small boy. He left me a fortune. I indulged myself and spent my time with fine food and drink in the company of good friends. For years I lived in this manner, until I awoke from my foolishness. I discovered that my fortune had gone. I was overcome with remorse when my money was all spent, and I realized that I could not escape my fate. Then I remembered the words that I had often heard my father speak when I was a child: 'Three things have precedence over three other things. The day of death over the day of birth, a live dog over a dead lion, and a grave over the finest of palaces.'

"Then I began to ponder what I should do. After much thought I sold whatever was left of my clothes, implements, and possessions. The proceeds amounted to about three thousand dinars. With this sum of money I began to trade. I had a desire to travel and see foreign lands and cities, and I remembered the words of a poet: 'He who would rise on high must work through many a night. He who would have pearls must dive to the depths of the sea, for only then can he achieve both esteem and wealth. But he who desires to rise and win esteem without the effort needed to acquire them will waste his life on wishes that cannot be fulfilled.'"

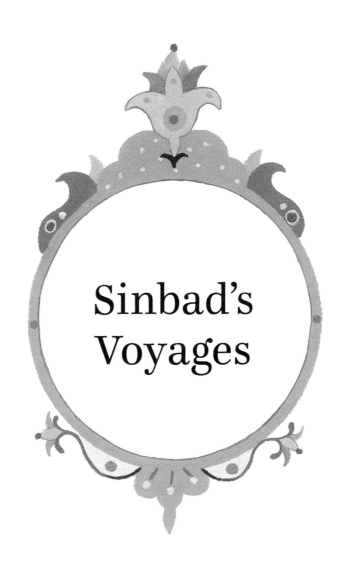

Sinbad's Voyages

Sinbad's First Voyage

I purchased all kinds of wares and had them brought to Basra, where I looked for a ship. Then we sailed from one island to another, from one ocean to another—and everywhere we sold our goods. All went well until we reached an island with trees around which there flew many birds proclaiming the oneness of God. The captain called upon his crew to take down the sails and to drop anchor. Everyone was cheerful, and we ate and drank upon the island. But while we were enjoying ourselves, suddenly the captain cried, "Look out, you travelers! Come swiftly to the ship; leave all your things behind and save your lives! The island on which you are sitting is nothing but a great fish, and as it now has too little water, it has to dive."

Even before the captain had finished speaking, the island began to move and to dive down in the midst of the ocean, so that all who were upon it went down under the water. I too sank into the waves, but God saved me from drowning by throwing a plank in my path. With relief in my heart I climbed upon it, and the wind then played with me in the wide ocean. The captain raised the sails and departed with what was left of the crew.

The next morning I was luckily thrown by a wave onto an island. The shores were so steep that one could not climb up them. I would have gone under the water had not one of the trees that stood along the coast stretched out its branches so far that I was able to grasp them. I clung to them with all my might, climbed them, and then jumped to the ground. I lay there until the following morning and awoke only when the sun had illuminated the island.

I stood up, walked around, ate some of the island fruits, and drank from its streams. Then I found a spring, and remained there for a day and a night. Sleep restored my strength, and I was able to move more easily. I walked among the trees and cut a stick on which I could lean.

All at once I saw something shining from a hilltop beside the sea. I headed toward it and came upon a horse that was bound to a tree. When it saw me, it neighed and stamped its hooves.

Then a man's voice said, "Who are you, and what land are you from?"

"I am a stranger. I was shipwrecked and found safety on this island."

When the man heard my story, he came out into the open, took my hand, and climbed down with me to a cave. Within was a large room, the floor of which was covered by a carpet. He bade me sit at the far end and brought me food.

My mind was reassured, and my fear abated. When he saw that I had satisfied my hunger and had rested, he asked me to tell him of my adventures. I told him my story from the very beginning until the present.

"Please do not be offended, sir, but now that I have told you all about myself, would you kindly tell me about your own situation, who you are and why you live here in such isolation?"

"I am King Mihrage's equerry, and I am in charge of all his stablemen. At the time of the new moon, we bring a thoroughbred mare here and bind her to the place you have seen, and then we hide in this cave. As soon as all is quiet, a sea stallion comes and mounts the mare, which he wishes to take back with him to the ocean. But as she is bound, he butts her with his head, kicks her with his hooves, and neighs loudly. As soon as we hear her cries, we rush out of the cave, and the stallion flees back to the sea. The mare then becomes pregnant by the stallion, and the foals are the finest horses, such as are possessed only by the sultans of the islands."

The equerry then continued, "It is fortunate that you have met us here. Otherwise, you would have found no one who could show you the way out of this place. You would have died here in sorrow, and no one would have known of your death."

While we were speaking, a horse suddenly rose out of the waves of the sea. He was larger than an ordinary horse and had more powerful hooves. He approached the mare, mounted her, and wanted to take her with him. Then the equerry and his stablemen shouted and ran out of the cave waving their spears, and the stallion fled back to the sea. The equerry untied the mare and let her run loose for a while. After that, we went ever onward until we reached the city of King Mihrage, who was pleased to see the approach of his horses. I was introduced to him, and he welcomed me and bade me tell my story.

The king was very impressed and said, "By God, now you shall begin a new life."

He gave me clothes, kept me close to him, and was so bountiful that he made me the guardian of all his coasts. I enjoyed the benefits of his generosity, looked after his business affairs, and profited from them myself. Whenever travelers came to the island, I would ask them about Baghdad; but none had been there, and none had even heard of Baghdad.

After I had been in the kingdom for some time, one day I went down as usual to the seashore and saw a ship landing. I stood and watched until its cargo had been unloaded, waiting to greet the crew. The captain came to me and said, "Sir, we still have goods on board whose owner we lost on an island. We do not know if he is still alive."

I asked him the name of the owner.

"His name is on his goods. It is Sinbad the Sailor, and he came from Baghdad."

Then the captain went on, "We therefore wish to sell his wares in accordance with their value and take the money to his family."

I now raised my voice and said to him, "I am Sinbad the Sailor, whom you discharged from your ship onto that island, together with many other merchants."

But the captain shook his head, was silent for a while, and then said, "There is no protection and no power besides that of God the Almighty. And there is no honesty left among men."

I asked him why he said this.

"Because you heard me say the name Sinbad, and I told you his whole story, and now you pretend that you are he so that you may take possession of his goods. By God, that is a sin! For I and all who were with me on the ship did with our own eyes see him drown."

I said, "Listen to my tale, and listen well! For lying is only for hypocrites." Then I reminded him of things that had taken place between him and me on the ship before we reached that island. When he heard these details from me and remembered our conversations, he became convinced that I was indeed Sinbad. He gave me all the goods that belonged to me. At once I opened a bale, took some precious objects out of it, and gave them to King Mihrage.

Then I sold the rest of my wares for a good profit, with which I bought other goods from the city, packed them, and took them to the ship. I bade farewell to King Mihrage, and by the grace of God we sailed away.

We were granted favorable winds and journeyed smoothly by day and by night, from island to island, from ocean to ocean, until we reached Basra. After a short stay there we traveled on to Baghdad. I took my goods to my own part of the city, greeted my friends and neighbors, bought my house back, and lived there with my relatives. Then I purchased slaves, both men and women, houses, and more goods. And so I regained the fortune I had squandered earlier.

Then Sinbad the Sailor said to Sinbad the Porter, "The night has fallen upon us. Your visit has brought us much pleasure. Stay with us for supper, and come again tomorrow so that I may tell you all that happened to me on my second voyage."

When supper was ended, Sinbad the Sailor ordered that a hundred dinars be handed to the porter, who gladly accepted them and went on his way with his load. He could hardly wait for the next day. When it dawned, he got up, washed, said his morning prayers, and went back to the house of Sinbad the Sailor. He wished him good morning, kissed the ground, and thanked him for his generosity. Then the sailor said to his guest, "Now, brother, you shall hear of my adventures on my second voyage."

Sinbad's
Second Voyage

One day when I was feeling very happy, I was suddenly seized once more by the desire to travel. I purchased goods that would be suitable to take on a voyage and embarked in the company of other merchants. After we had prayed to God for his blessing, we raised anchor and sailed away. We went from island to island, from land to land, from city to city; saw all the sights; and did profitable business.

Soon, however, fate threw us onto an unknown island. The captain dropped anchor, and we voyagers disembarked. The island was rich in fruits, flowers, and birds but so deserted that we could find neither dwelling place nor fellow human being. I sat down beside a spring and bade a slave bring me some food. After I had eaten and drunk, I fell asleep. When I awoke, there was no sign of the ship, and I found myself all alone. Then I was overcome by a feeling of great sorrow. I regretted having once more put to sea. But finally I entrusted myself to the will of God.

I wandered around for a while and then climbed a tree from which I could look out on all sides. After a while I noticed something white. I climbed down from the tree and walked in that direction. Even from a distance I could see that it was a large ball. I approached and touched it, and it felt as soft as silk. I walked around it, looking for an opening.

Suddenly the heavens darkened as if covered by a black cloud. And now I saw a bird of extraordinary size. I recalled that the sailors had often spoken of a giant bird that they called a roc, and I suspected that the large ball that had so astonished me was its egg. Then indeed it spread its great feathers and settled down upon the egg.

21

When the bird sat upon it and stretched out its legs, I stood and bound myself to it with my turban. For I thought, Perhaps the bird will carry me to a land with cities and people, away from this deserted island. Throughout the night I remained still and silent.

The following morning the bird flew away, bearing me up into the clouds until I could discern nothing below. Then it flew down from the heights at such speed that I lost consciousness. However, when it landed upon the earth, I swiftly untied my turban.

When I had recovered, I looked around my new location and found myself in a valley that was surrounded on all sides by rocks so steep that they could not be climbed. When I walked on a little, I saw that the ground was covered with diamonds. The whole valley was swarming with snakes.

Soon I came to a cave and went inside. I blocked the entrance with a large boulder. But when I looked around the cave, I discovered a snake that was lying on eggs the size of elephants. I could not sleep that night out of fear, but I stayed calm and kept myself awake until daybreak.

Then I pushed the boulder aside, went out, and wandered around. Suddenly a large piece of meat fell to the ground from above. I remembered what a merchant had told me once. Merchants used a trick to get hold of the diamonds. They threw fresh meat into the valley, and the gems stuck to the meat. And so when an eagle took the meat and flew up into the hills again, the merchants would rush toward it and with their loud cries force it to let go of the meat and fly away. Then they would pluck the diamonds from the meat and take them away.

I began to collect diamonds and to pack them in a bag. Then I took the meat and tied it tightly to my chest with my turban. Soon an eagle came and seized in its claws the piece of meat to which I had attached myself. It carried me to the top of the hill and was about to eat the meat. However, the merchants who had been hiding nearby now shouted and screamed in order to frighten the eagle away from its meat. I swiftly freed myself and stood up. One of the merchants approached, looking for diamonds, but was startled when he saw me.

"Do not be afraid, brother. I am a man like yourself, and I have come here in a miraculous manner. You shall not suffer any loss, for I have many diamonds and will give you more than you would have found within this meat."

Now all the other merchants gathered around me. They told me that each of them had thrown meat into the valley, and they showed me the diamonds that they had obtained. I pulled a handful out of my bag and gave them to the owner of the piece of meat to which I had tied myself.

The remaining diamonds I sold to the other merchants. Then I traveled with them from land to land and from city to city, doing business as I went.

Among the many islands that we visited, there was one upon which grew the camphor tree. This is so thick and has such dense foliage that a hundred people may find shade in its shadow. The liquid that the camphor produces flows out of an opening that one makes in the tree with a spear. It looks like milk and immediately thickens like rubber. Once the liquid has been released, the tree withers and dies.

On this same island were rhinoceroses: animals that were bigger and stronger than elephants, and grazed like buffalo. They had a long horn as thick as a date palm. One traveler described to me how the rhinoceros fights with the elephant, piercing the elephant's body with its horn and carrying it away on its head. But then the giant roc swoops down, grasps them both in its talons, carries them to its nest, and feeds its chicks with them.

After this and other adventures, we finally reached Basra. We stayed there for a few days and then went on to Baghdad. My family was happy at my return, and my friends congratulated me.

Thus did Sinbad the Sailor end the tale of his second voyage. He gave the porter another hundred dinars and invited him to return the following day to hear the account of his third voyage.

Sinbad's Third Voyage

Let me tell you, dear friends, that after living a life of luxury for some time in Baghdad, once more I felt the desire to travel. For humans always yearn for something different. And so I bought many goods to take on a voyage, forgot my earlier sufferings, went to Basra, and walked along the seashore.

There I saw a large ship on which were some well-respected merchants. I had my goods taken aboard, and the merchants were pleased to have my company. With God's blessing, our voyage passed without any misfortune, and we made large profits.

One day when we were sailing quite contentedly on a surging sea, the captain suddenly uttered a cry of despair, struck himself in the face, tore the hairs from his beard, and ripped his clothing. "Oh, merchants! We are all doomed!"

When we asked what was the matter, he answered, "I must tell you that the violent storms have driven us off course, and our misfortune is that it has brought us to the Isle of the Apes. No man has ever left this island alive."

The captain dropped anchor and took down the sails. Soon the apes came, and climbed on board the ship from all sides in such numbers that we could neither kill them nor drive them away. They bit through the anchor cable and the ropes of the sails, pulled the ship to the shore, made us leave, and then disappeared with the ship along with everything that was on it.

Without knowing what might become of us, we wandered around the island, feeding ourselves on its plants. Suddenly in the distance there appeared a building, and as we drew near, we saw that it was a

lofty castle that had a large gate with two wings of ebony. We entered and found ourselves in a courtyard with piles of dry, green wood. This all seemed very strange to us, but we stayed in the castle, where there was no sign of any human being.

While we were resting, suddenly the earth shook. With a roar like that of a raging storm, a human figure as big as a palm tree appeared before us. He had red eyes, a broad face, and a big mouth. At the sight of this monster we scattered.

We did not dare to join one another again until God brought us the morning light and the giant went on his way. Only then did we gather together and decide either to find a hiding place on the island or to escape. However, we could not find any secure spot, and so we returned to the castle. Then one of us said, "My friends, let us devise a means of killing this monster and making ourselves safe."

The other merchants agreed to this suggestion, but I said, "First let us use the wood to build ourselves a raft. If we succeed in killing the giant, then let God decide what should happen next. But if not, let us board the raft, row out to sea, and entrust ourselves to God's hands."

At once we carried the wood to the shore, together with ropes that we had found near the castle and all kinds of rags, and with these we tied the pieces of wood together to make the raft solid. Then we returned to the castle. Soon the giant arrived, together with two more of his kind, who were even bigger and more hideous than himself.

When we saw him approaching the castle with his arms around the shoulders of his two companions, we hastened to the raft and tried to row away from the shore. The giants saw us, armed themselves with large stones, and ran to the shore. They threw the stones at us, and many of us were struck and killed, while others fell into the sea.

Before long I was the sole survivor. I found myself alone on the high seas, a toy for the winds and waves to play with. And yet despite my suffering, I did not cease to row with all my might and main. Eventually the wind blew me to an island, where I went ashore, fell to the ground, and slept a deep slumber.

The following morning I wanted to throw myself into the sea, but my inner self fought against it, for man still cherishes life. And so I set forth, ate some fruit, and climbed a hill, from which I caught sight of a ship amid the waves. I shouted at the top of my voice and waved with a

branch I broke from a tree. The crew saw me at once, and the ship came close to the shore.

The people asked me who I was. "I am a man," I replied, "so please take me aboard, and I will tell you how I came to be here."

They brought me food, and when I had regained some strength, I told them the tale of my ordeal, from my departure to the moment when I boarded their ship. They were amazed by my story, took my foul-smelling clothes off me, threw them into the sea, and bought me clean raiment as well as various foods and fresh water. And so I was blessed with new life after I had almost given way to despair.

We now journeyed on with favorable winds until we finally came to Salahat, where sandalwood comes from, and we anchored in the port of this island. My traveling companions began to unload their goods in order to sell them. In the meantime, the captain called me to him and said, "Listen, sir. You are a stranger and you are poor, and you have told us of your sufferings. Therefore I would like to do you a good turn." I answered that I was now in great need, and he should do what seemed right to him. He continued, "Know that on this ship are wares that belonged to a merchant from Baghdad who journeyed with us for many years but whom we then lost. We wished to sell his goods, collect the money, and on our return give it to his heirs. But you should sell them and in return claim a suitable sum that will enable you to live during your travels."

I thanked God, said nothing, and controlled myself until all the goods had been unloaded. Then I turned to the captain and asked him to tell me more about the owner of these goods. When he told me that they

31

had left the owner on an island because they had completely forgotten about him, and when he then spoke my name, my joy was unbounded and I cried, "Oh, captain, oh, merchants! By God, I am Sinbad the Sailor! The goods belong to me, and the merchants will be my witnesses!"

Then the captain said, "How can you claim such a thing?"

He did not believe me. Soon all the others gathered around us, and some believed me while others thought me to be a liar. Then one merchant stepped out from their midst, greeted me, and said, "You have spoken the truth, Sinbad the Sailor. This money and these goods belong to you."

He continued, "I told you all recently about the strangest thing that ever happened to me on my travels. When once I was collecting diamonds and threw pieces of meat down from the hills, there was a man tied to one of those pieces of meat. That was Sinbad, who gave me many diamonds from a bag that was full of them. We traveled together to Basra, from where he continued his journey to Baghdad. I do not know what has happened to him since then, but I thank God that he is here among us now."

After he had spoken these words, he provided the captain with further evidence so that he no longer doubted me and once more bade me welcome: "May God be praised for your rescue."

Thereupon my goods were restored to me, and I went on to sell them for an unusually large profit.

From the island of Salahat we sailed to India, where I bought cloves, ginger, and other spices. From there we sailed to Sind, where again we bought and sold goods and saw the sights of the land. On this journey I saw many strange things, including fish as big as steer and birds that came forth from conches, and laid and hatched their eggs on the water.

At last, after this long voyage, I returned to Basra and from there to Baghdad. I gave many presents to my relatives, friends, and acquaintances; gave clothes to orphans and widows; and again bought slaves, both men and women. I lived in comfort and thought no more of the sufferings I had endured. And that is the end of my third voyage.

Sinbad then sent for food, again gave the porter a hundred dinars, and said, "Come back tomorrow. Then you shall hear of the even stranger experiences I endured during my fourth voyage."

The porter promised to come and went home full of amazement at the tales told by Sinbad. The next day he went there once more. When everyone was present, they feasted as they had done the previous day, and then Sinbad began his next account.

Sinbad's Fourth Voyage

For a while I indulged in all of life's pleasures, and my excessive happiness and success in business enabled me to forget all the trials and tribulations of the past. One day, however, I received a visit from some merchants, who told me about their various journeys and reawakened my desire to travel. My decision was swift, and I bought goods suitable for maritime trade, then boarded a large ship together with some of my friends.

We had been sailing for quite a while when one day we ran into a gale that forced the captain to lower the sails and drop anchor. However, the storm then attacked us from the front, broke the anchor cable, and blew down the mast. The ship sank, and many of the passengers drowned.

A few others and I were fortunate enough to cling to some driftwood and when the wind abated were able to paddle on for a while with our hands and feet. But then the storm rose again, and, by God's will, the waves took us to a large island. We went ashore, ate some plants, and spent the night resting on the strand.

When the sun sent down its first rays, we left the shore and began to explore the island. We saw some huts; and as we approached them, a man came out, took hold of us, and led us inside.

We were given some food that none of us knew or had ever seen before. My friends, weak with hunger, began to eat it, but I had a feeling of revulsion and despite my hunger refused even to taste it. That was my good fortune. For shortly afterward I saw that my friends had lost all reason and went on eating like madmen.

It was soon clear to me that our hosts were cannibals who would fatten every stranger and then hand him to their chief to devour. I refrained from all food and drink, even though I was now wasting away.

The cannibals perceived my condition and took no further notice of me. And so one day I was able to leave their huts and escape. I came to a broad road and decided to follow it. I was still afraid of being pursued and so I ran for a while, then proceeded more slowly. Finally when night fell, I lay down, although fear prevented me from sleeping. So I rose again and went on through the night, rested once more in the morning, ate some fruit to give me strength, and continued my journey for seven days.

On the eighth day I saw a group of people close to the seashore. They immediately approached me and asked who I was and where I came from. I began to tell them my story and to describe the terrors I had experienced. They interrupted me and asked what miracle had enabled me to escape from the cannibals, and I told them everything from start to finish. They were amazed by my story and brought me some food. When I had eaten and rested, I went with them on board their ship, and we sailed to the island from which they had come.

There they took me to their king, who welcomed me and asked me to tell him my story. When I had finished, he congratulated me, bade me sit down, and sent for food. I praised God, thanked the king for his benevolence, and stayed in his capital city. My time there comforted me after all my misfortunes, and the kindness that the king bestowed upon me brought me much contentment.

In this land I noticed something that seemed to me most unusual. Everyone rode the finest horses without stirrups or saddles. One day I asked the king why he did not use a saddle. He replied that I was speaking of things he had never heard of.

I went at once to a carpenter and taught him to make a saddle in accordance with a sketch that I drew. When it was ready, I went to see the king, chose one of his best horses, put the saddle and bridle on it, and asked him to mount the horse. He took great pleasure in the device, and showed his gratitude by giving me many presents. I then made different saddles for other important people in the kingdom, and they too gave me so many presents that I soon became a rich man.

One day the king said to me, "Sinbad, I have high esteem for you, and I know that all my subjects feel the same. I have a request to make of you, and you must promise to grant it."

"Your Majesty," I replied, "tell me what you want me to do."

He said, "It is my wish that you take one of the noblest daughters of my city to be your wife so that she binds you to us and makes you one of us. I shall ensure that you have sufficient income to live without any financial cares."

As I did not dare to refuse, I replied, "It is for you to command, Your Majesty!"

He summoned the judge and married me to a beautiful woman who had both money and goods. Then he gave me a dwelling place and slaves, and arranged a salary for me. I was happy and thought, I must do God's will. If he desires to send me home, no one can prevent it.

However, I soon grew to love my wife, and was loved by her, so that for a while we lived happily together. But one day I heard a cry from my neighbor's house, and when I asked for the cause, I learned that his wife had died.

I considered it my duty to visit him. "May God give you strength and prosperity, have mercy on the deceased, and grant you long life."

"Alas!" he cried. "What good can your wishes do me? I have but an hour to live! I shall never see you or my friends again until the Day of Resurrection."

"Why is that?" I asked.

"You should know," he replied, "that my wife will now be washed and dressed, and I shall be buried

with her. That is the custom of our people. The living man shall be buried with his dead wife, and the living wife with her dead husband, so that even after death they remain united."

I cried, "By God, that is a terrible custom that no one would willingly obey!"

While we were talking, many of the inhabitants of the city came to offer their condolences to the bereaved. The corpse was laid in a coffin and taken to a mountain at the far end of the island, where a large stone covered the entrance to an underground cavern.

The stone was raised, and then both the corpse and the living man were lowered on a rope. The man was given a jug of water and seven loaves of bread. Then the entrance to the tomb was closed again.

Afterward I went to the king and asked, "Your Majesty, how can you bury people alive?"

He replied, "That is our custom. And that was the custom among our fathers and our forefathers and all the kings before us."

I asked, "Does this law apply also to foreigners?"

"Most certainly," he replied. "They are not exempt."

The fear that my wife might die before me and that I would be buried alive with her filled me with dark thoughts. I soon began to detest my life in this city. But then in time I calmed myself and thought, Perhaps I shall die before my wife, or God will help me to return home before she dies. However, after a while she became ill, and then she died.

Many people came to comfort me and my wife's relatives. The king also came to offer me his condolences. My wife was washed and dressed and borne in a coffin to the mountain, where the stone was lifted from the entrance to the cavern and the last farewells were spoken.

I cried, "Does God permit you to bury a foreigner alive? I did not know your custom! Otherwise I would never have married one of your women!"

But they did not listen to me. They bound me fast and lowered me into the cavern. Then they closed the entrance. The custom was to dress the deceased in the finest robes and jewelry, and this they did also for my wife. She was bedecked with gems and precious stones.

There was a chink of light from somewhere; and when all the people had gone, I looked around the cavern, which stank abominably, for it was filled with the dead. There is no protection and no power besides

that of God the Almighty. Only why did I have to be married in this city? By God, I had survived one disaster only to be plunged into another.

Night fell, and it was dark and terrible in this place. I was hungry and thirsty and ate a little bread, drank some water, and then lay still through the night. I was awakened by a soft sound. Some animal perhaps? I stood up and followed the sound until I saw a light. As I drew nearer, I discovered that it came from an opening that led to the sea. When I was certain that this was so, I at once became calm and envisaged the beginning of a new life. I squeezed through the opening and found myself on the seashore.

I thanked God for saving me and went back into the cavern. I took as many of the diamonds, pearls, and rubies as I could carry. No sooner had I once more left the cavern than I saw a ship sailing by.

I shouted as loudly as I could and waved a piece of cloth. They saw me and sent a boat to the shore. The sailors asked who I was and how I had come to this place, where they had never before seen any human being. I told them that I was a merchant who had been shipwrecked and had managed somehow to make my way here. But I said nothing about what had befallen me in the city and in the cavern. I was afraid that there might be someone from the city on the ship.

When I went aboard, I repeated my story and added that I had no money but only some jewels that I had managed to save from the shipwreck. I offered some of these to the captain in gratitude for his having rescued me. But he said he took all shipwrecked people on board to honor God. And indeed he took good care of me until we reached Basra, from where after a short stay I continued my journey home to Baghdad. I shared my treasures with my family and friends, and gave to the poor and to orphans. Once again I spent a period of time enjoying the pleasures of life with my friends.

"Those, then, were the adventures I experienced on my fourth voyage. But come again tomorrow," said Sinbad the Sailor to the porter, "and I will tell you about my fifth voyage."

Once more he gave him a hundred dinars, and the following morning when the porter returned and they had all eaten and drunk, he began the following tale.

Sinbad's Fifth Voyage

The pleasures of life cast such a spell on me that I quickly forgot the perils and sufferings I had endured. Once more I felt driven to visit foreign lands. I bought goods and journeyed to Basra.

When I came to the seashore, I saw a large ship upon which were many merchants. I bought it, and hired a captain and crew. We read the first sura of the Koran and with God's blessing set sail, voyaging from city to city and from land to land, until fate drove us to a desert island. Here we found the egg of a roc, which from a distance looked like a great dome. The chick was in the process of hatching, for its beak was already visible.

The merchants who had accompanied me on the voyage now began to strike the egg with stones. I shouted to them not to touch it, because otherwise the bird would destroy our ship, but they paid no heed to my words. They smashed the egg and took out the chick.

Soon it was as if the sun had been covered by a black cloud. When we looked up at the sky, we saw that the supposed cloud was in fact the wings of the roc that was circling above the egg. We hastened away from the shore and back to the ship.

In the meantime, the roc examined the egg, and when he saw that it was broken, he let out a terrible cry. Then he and his mate followed us and were soon hovering over our ship. We saw that they both had huge boulders in their talons, and the male dropped his toward us. But the helmsman swiftly turned our vessel in a different direction. Hardly had we escaped from this danger, with God's help, than the female roc dropped her even bigger boulder directly onto our ship, which was smashed to pieces.

43

All the passengers and all the crew drowned. I alone was able to cling to a piece of the wreckage. For three days I paddled with my hands and feet until at last I reached an island.

I was half dead with hunger and exhaustion. After I had slept for a while and regained my strength, I wandered around and found an abundance of birds, streams, and fruit trees. I ate and drank until I was full and then in the evening lay down to rest, though fearful because I had found no trace of any fellow humans.

The next day, however, when I had penetrated farther inland, I came upon an old man sitting beside a water wheel. I thought that perhaps he might be a stranger like myself, and I approached. He returned my greeting and bade me welcome. I asked him who he was and where he came from, and where exactly we were. He merely responded with signs to indicate that I should carry him across the stream that drove his water wheel.

I assumed that his physical condition was such that he needed help and so I took him upon my back and carried him to the place he had indicated. But then I could no longer get him off my shoulders, for he had wound his legs tightly around my neck.

When I saw what new disaster had befallen me, I cried, "There is no protection and no power besides that of God the Almighty, but no sooner have I become free from one evil than I am plunged into another!"

My heart was filled with fear, and the world turned black before my eyes. I lost consciousness and fell like a dead man to the ground. The old man loosened his grip a little, and on regaining consciousness I was able to breathe and rest. I could feel that his legs had cut into my neck as deeply as if he had lashed me with a whip. Now he ordered me to carry him around under the trees. He ate the fruits of these trees, and neither by night nor by day did he release his hold on my neck. Even when he slept his grip was so tight that I could not free myself.

One day I came upon some gourds that were lying on the ground. I took one that had dried, hollowed it out, and pressed the juice from some grapes into it. Then I closed the opening and laid the gourd in the sun so that the juice would turn into wine. I drank some, and it not only gave me strength, but it also intoxicated me sufficiently for me to feel no more weariness. On one occasion I became so cheered by the wine

that I began to sing, recite poetry, and dance hither and thither with the old man on my shoulders.

When he saw its effects, he indicated to me that he also wanted to partake. I passed the gourd to him, and he emptied it to the last drop. He became very cheerful, clapped his hands, and loosened his legs. All his limbs were trembling, and he was completely overcome. Then I pried his legs from my neck, set him down upon the earth, and celebrated the fact that he was still unconscious. I took my chance and fled.

I went back to the seashore, ate more of the island's fruits, and kept watch for potential rescuers. Great was my joy when one day a ship came sailing by and anchored off the island. When the crew came ashore, I approached them and greeted them.

Soon they had all gathered around me. After I had told my story, the captain said, "He is known as the Old Man of the Sea, and no one has ever escaped from him alive." They congratulated me on my escape, gave me food and clothing, and took me on board.

After a few days, the ship was driven by winds to a city that had a castle surrounded by walls with an iron-studded gate. Every evening the people of the city came out through this gate and went to the shore, where they climbed into their boats. They would spend the night far out at sea. They feared that apes would come from the mountains at night and attack them.

While I was wandering around the city, the ship sailed away, and I bitterly regretted having left it; but my regret served no purpose now. When a man from the city saw me lost in thought, he said, "You appear to be a stranger."

I replied, "I am indeed, and now I am alone, unfamiliar with both the city and its people."

The man responded, "Do not fear. Come with me to my boat, because if you stay the night in the city, you will be killed."

I followed him and climbed into his boat, which took us about a mile offshore, and not until morning did we return to the city.

Throughout the day everyone went about his business. But the man asked me, "Are you master of no craft?"

I replied, "By God, I am no craftsman. I was a rich merchant but I lost everything in a shipwreck."

Then I told him my whole story. When he had listened to it with amazement, he handed me a cotton sack full of stones. "Take this sack and follow me."

He led me to a group of men and said, "This man is a stranger who has suffered a shipwreck, has no possessions left, and knows no craft. Take him with you and teach him your trade. Perhaps he will earn so much that he will be able to return to his homeland."

They answered, "By our heads and eyes we shall do it."

Then the man said, "Do as they do, and when you return, come to me again."

He gave me some more food and then he left. I thanked him and joined the others. They took me to a place where there were trees so tall that no man could climb them. Beneath them lay many apes, but as soon as they saw us, they climbed the trees. Then the men took stones from their bags and threw them at the monkeys, who in anger plucked fruits from the trees and threw them down at us. When I looked more closely, I saw that the fruits were coconuts.

I also took stones out of my sack and threw them at the apes. They pelted me with nuts, which I collected in large numbers. We spent the whole day in this manner. When we returned to the city in the evening, I gave the man all that I had collected. He was pleased and said, "Go with those people every day and bring what God has bestowed upon you."

I thanked him and continued to collect coconuts.

One day a ship dropped anchor before the city, and on it were many merchants who had come to exchange their goods. I went to my host and told him that I would like to leave on this ship. He went to see the captain, paid my fare, gave me some food, and took his leave.

I boarded the ship with many coconuts, and we sailed from island to island until we came to another large city. There I exchanged my coconuts for cloves and pepper, and saw a pepper tree. I was told that it bore large bunches, and beside each bunch grew a large leaf that gave it shade and protected it against the rain.

We also went to other islands where we found eaglewood, whose trees have their roots in the sea. The inhabitants were given over to wine and indecent conduct, and knew nothing of prayer.

Then we came to the island of the pearl divers. I gave them coconuts and bade them dive for me, putting my trust in God. They brought me many precious pearls, and I became richer than ever before. And so we sailed on and on until we reached Basra.

Here I rested for several days. Then I journeyed on to Baghdad and my family and friends, whom I had feared I would never see again. Once more I was able to enjoy the pleasures of life and soon forgot all my sufferings.

"Those, then, were the adventures I experienced on my fifth voyage," said Sinbad the Sailor, ending his tale. Again he gave one hundred dinars to Sinbad the Porter and invited him to return the following morning in order to hear what had happened during the sixth voyage.

Sinbad's Sixth Voyage

After I had enjoyed a time of great happiness and had become ever richer, some merchants came to me and talked of their travels. And so once more I was overcome by the desire to set forth and explore foreign lands. I bought wares suitable to take on a voyage and journeyed to Basra. Here I found a large ship aboard which there were many merchants.

By the grace of God I sailed with them from ocean to ocean, from island to island, from city to city; did good business everywhere; and was very content. But one day the captain suddenly shouted to his sailors, struck himself in the face, threw off his turban, and plucked his beard: "Oh misery! My house will be desolate! My children will be orphans!"

We ran to him and asked, "What has happened?"

"We cannot escape from this mountain. We have lost our way, and fate has driven us to a place which no man has ever left alive. But pray to God, for perhaps there is one pure soul among you whose prayer he will grant."

We began to pray, and the captain climbed the mast to see if there was anywhere we could turn. But he found no means of diverting the ship. He climbed down and in his grief fell unconscious onto the deck. Soon after, a wind blew us toward the mountain. The ship turned full circle, crashed into the rocks, and was smashed to pieces. Many of the passengers, myself included, clung to the side of the mountain and managed to climb it.

When we reached the top, we saw an island full of large trees. On its shores lay the goods and relics of wrecked ships. I walked on with the others until we came to an underground stream that flowed from the mountain. We drank the water, went on, but became ever weaker, for our only food was plants.

Whenever one of us died, we washed him, wrapped him in his clothes, and buried him on the shore. Our numbers dwindled. Soon there were but three of us, and finally I was the only one left alive.

The Almighty God then put a thought into my head. The stream that ran underground had to emerge somewhere in the open. If I built a raft and entrusted myself to the flow of the water, with the help of God I might be saved—or else I would perish. I built my raft from the timbers and ropes that lay strewn about the shore, and I loaded it with pearls, precious stones, amber, eaglewood, and plants for food. I stepped aboard the raft with two small oars, asked the Almighty for his blessing, and delivered myself to the course of the stream.

Down in the caverns, I could no longer see daylight, and the stream bore me along without my knowing where. I traveled for days in the darkness, and never saw a single ray of light. At times the roofs of the caverns were so low that I came close to injuring my head. And in many places the stream became so narrow that I had to lay the oars upon the raft. I began to rue the action I had taken, and in my fear of death I barely noticed my hunger and thirst. And so it went on. Now I slept, now I awoke, now the stream narrowed, now it broadened, and meanwhile the current carried my raft ever onward.

At last, from sheer weakness and hunger, I fell into a deep slumber. When I awoke, I found myself in a field, surrounded by a crowd of Indians. They talked to me, but I could not understand their language. However, at this moment I was so overjoyed that I did not know whether I was awake or dreaming. I recited the words of the poet: "'Leave Destiny to run its course, and let thy mind be still. For as thou tremblest, God hath changed all things to suit his will.'"

One of the men who saw that I was unable to answer said in Arabic, "May the peace of God be with you."

I replied, "May God's peace and blessing be with you."

Then he told me, "We cultivate the field and have come to water it from the river. We saw your raft, moored it, and waited till you awoke. Tell us who you are and where you are from."

I asked them first to give me something to eat, for otherwise I would starve to death. They brought me food with which I was able to satisfy my hunger, and so when I felt stronger and calmer, I told them all that had happened to me, while the man who had spoken to me acted as my interpreter. As soon as I finished, they said they would take me to see their king.

They surrounded me again and carried both myself and my raft, on which were all my precious stones, pearls, and amber. When I appeared before the king, he welcomed me and asked about my circumstances, whereupon I repeated my story through my interpreter.

The king was astonished by my adventure and honored me, and in return I gave him gifts of pearls and precious stones. He took my gifts, sent for food and drink, and offered me a room in his palace. There I lived a life of privilege, and told him about my home and about the rule of Harun al Rashid, which gained me even greater esteem.

One day I heard that there were some merchants traveling to Basra. I resolved to join them and hoped the king would commend me to them. I went to him, kissed the ground at his feet, and informed him of my decision. Then indeed he commended me to the merchants, and gave me many gifts and provisions for the journey. Trusting in God, we embarked and sailed from ocean to ocean, from island to island, until by God's grace we reached Basra, from where after a few days I continued my journey to Baghdad.

My family had long given me up for dead, and they were overjoyed at my homecoming. Once more I gave gifts to them and to my friends, as well as to the poor. The caliph himself heard that I had returned and sent for me.

I kissed the ground before him and gave him precious stones that were worthy of him. He accepted my gift and bade me tell him all that had happened to me on my journey. He listened with astonishment, and then he summoned his secretary to write down my story and to keep it in the treasure chamber so that all might learn from it.

And so again I lived in Baghdad enjoying the pleasures of life and soon forgot all my sufferings.

"Now you have heard my adventures during my sixth voyage. Come again tomorrow," said Sinbad the Sailor to Sinbad the Porter, "and I shall tell you about my seventh and final voyage."

Once again he gave the porter a hundred dinars. The following day when the porter returned and together with the other friends had eaten and drunk, Sinbad the Sailor began as follows.

Sinbad's
Last Voyage

After another period of living most pleasantly in Baghdad, I was once more overcome by the desire to travel. I bought all kinds of goods, packed them in bales, and, trusting blindly in God's guidance, journeyed to Basra. Here I found a large ship full of reputable merchants, and I went aboard to join them.

When we had traveled a fair distance, we were assailed by a heavy storm. It rained so hard that we covered our goods with all kinds of garments and cloths, and prayed to God to protect us against the dangers. The captain, however, tied a rope around himself and climbed the mast to scan the ocean around us. Then he struck his own face, threw off his turban, and tore the hairs from his beard, crying, "Pray to God to save you! Weep for your lives and bid one another farewell!"

We asked him what had happened, and he replied, "We have lost our way, and soon the wind will have blown us to the farthest edge of the world."

Hardly had he spoken these words when the ship was struck by a violent gust of wind. We bade one another farewell, said our final prayers, and gave ourselves up to the will of God.

Now three giant fish swam toward us and surrounded our ship. The biggest of them opened wide its jaws to swallow the whole ship, for its mouth was as huge as a city gate. But a second gust raised the ship up high, and then it crashed down upon another fish and was shattered to pieces so that all of us fell into the sea.

However, God in his mercy gave me a large plank to cling to, and I climbed onto it. At last the wind and waves carried me to the shores of an island. I reproached myself bitterly: "My earlier voyages have taught me nothing. Whenever I was in peril, I swore never to leave home again. And so by God I deserve what has now befallen me."

I wept for a long time, begged God to be merciful, and called upon him to be my witness: "If I am saved now, I shall never more leave home and never more talk of travel."

I wandered along the shore, recalling the words of the poet:
"When things entangle and in a knot do tighten,
Heaven's words new clearness will produce.
Have patience! What was dark will one day lighten,
And he who tied the knot may make it loose."

Soon the idea came to me to build a little raft and put to sea on it. I thought, If I am rescued, then it will be by divine providence. If I die, then my sufferings will be at an end. And so I collected wood and planks from other wrecked ships, tore my garments into strips, and made ropes out of them with which to bind the boards together.

I pulled the raft into the sea and rowed for three days without any food or drink. Fear prevented me from sleeping. On the fourth day I came to a high mountain from which water flowed down to the earth. Here I stopped, saying to myself, "There is no protection and no power besides that of God the Almighty. If only you had stayed where you were, you would have had dates and other plants to eat. Instead you must die here."

It was impossible to return, for I could not stop the raft in its course, as the river carried it beneath the mountain. I lay down, but the raft was so narrow that my sides and back often scraped against the walls of the caverns.

After some time, with God's help, I emerged from under the mountain into a valley. The water still thundered down, but I clung to my raft, which was flung left and right at the whim of the waves. The wind and current carried the raft along until fate brought me to a city.

As I was unable to stop the raft, the people there threw a large net over it and pulled me to dry land. I was naked and as thin as a skeleton. An old man came toward me, gave me a robe, and took me to his home. His people made me welcome and brought me food. Then a slave brought some warm water with which I washed my hands. They took me to a place at the side of their house, and here I was served by another slave. I spent three days there.

On the fourth day the old man came and said to me, "You are welcome here, for the year has been blessed by your coming."

I replied, "May God preserve you and reward you for the kindness you have shown me."

Then he said to me, "Know, my son, that while you have been here as our guest, I have had my servants bring your wares onto the land so that they may be dried. Would you now like to come with me to the market and sell them?"

I did not know what to say in reply, for I had brought no wares. But I replied, "My father, you know what is best to be done."

At the market I was greeted by the traders, who congratulated me on my rescue. I discovered at once that by "wares" the old man had meant the boards and planks I had collected on the island. When the broker came to sell the wood, the merchants' bids rose to 10,000 dinars.

The old man said to me, "My son, that is the current worth of your wares. If you wish, you may sell them. But if you are willing to wait for a while, you will get a higher price for them."

I said, "I shall do as you think best."

He replied, "Then I shall give you a hundred dinars more if you sell the wood to me."

I agreed to his offer, and he had the wood taken to his store. He also gave me 10,100 dinars and a box with a lock. I was to put the money in it and carry the key with me, for I would not need to spend any of the money so long as I was a guest in his home.

After some time he said to me, "I would like to make a proposal to you. I am a rich man, but I have no son. I do, however, have a young daughter. I want you to marry her, remain here with me, and be my son. Then I will leave my entire fortune to you."

I could not say anything, for such bounty somehow made me ashamed. However, he continued, "Do what pleases you. You can marry my daughter, or stay here as you are, or return home with your possessions."

I could only answer, "Sire, do as you will with your humble servant. You have been like a father to me."

Thereupon he sent for the cadi and for witnesses, and married me to his daughter. She was richly adorned with necklaces, jewels, and gold rings that must have been worth a thousand dinars. It was impossible even to guess at the value of her clothes. I lived happily with her. Her

father put me in charge of all his property, and I was like a native of the city.

One day, though, I discovered that whenever the moon was full, there were people who grew wings and changed their form. They flew high into the sky, and only the children remained at home. When once more the moon was full, I took hold of one and said, "You must take me with you."

He took me on his back and flew with me so high that I heard the angels praising God. I cried, "May God be praised!"

But hardly had I spoken these words when a blazing fire fell from the sky upon the flying people so that they fled, almost burned to death. The one who was carrying me threw me angrily onto the top of a mountain and disappeared. I bitterly regretted what I had done to myself and said, "There is no protection and no power besides that of God the Almighty! But as often as God is merciful to me and frees me from one perilous situation, I plunge myself into another."

I was descending the side of the mountain when I met two youths with shining faces, each of whom was carrying a golden staff in his hand. I approached them and greeted them: "In the name of God I ask, who are you?"

They replied, "We are hermits who live upon this mountain and pray to God."

They gave me a staff like their own and went on their way.

Suddenly a great snake came out from under the mountain, carrying a man in its jaws. Only his head was visible, and he cried, "Whoever frees me from this snake will receive God's protection against all disaster!"

I hit the snake with the golden staff, and it spat out the man and disappeared. Then the man said to me, "Because you have saved me, I shall be your companion and will always be by your side."

I bade him welcome and walked with him for a while upon the mountain.

Suddenly we were approached by a crowd of people. Among them was the man who had carried me on his back. I greeted him and asked, "Do brothers proceed thus against brothers?"

The man answered, "Friend, you almost condemned us to death and destruction by saying the name of God."

I asked for forgiveness, and he agreed to take me once more on his back. However, I had to accept the condition that I must not call upon God again. I gave the golden staff to the man I had rescued from the snake and bade him farewell. Soon afterward I arrived home on the back of my new compatriot.

My wife was relieved to welcome me home, and when I told her what had happened, she informed me that the winged men were devils who had renounced God. She and her father were of a different race. But then she went on, "My father is dead, and we have no other family here, so let us sell our goods and go to your home."

I agreed and waited for a favorable opportunity.

One day I heard that a number of foreigners who were living in the city wished to depart and so they had built a large ship. I went to them, and bought a place for myself and my wife. We took all the possessions we could, left the rest behind, and boarded the ship. We sailed from island to island, and from ocean to ocean, until by the grace of God we reached Basra. We did not linger there but came straight to Baghdad, the city of peace.

Praise be to God that he has reunited me with my friends, of whom, Sinbad the Porter, you are now one.

So ends the story of Sinbad the Sailor.

SAID went to Munich in 1965, at the age of seventeen, to study political science. After the downfall of the shah in 1979, he returned briefly to Iran, but the newly established theocracy of the mullahs caused him to seek exile once more in Germany. He writes poetry and prose in German, having mastered all its nuances, and he feels "at home" in the language. From 1995 until 1996 he was vice president and from 2000 until 2002 president of the PEN Centre in Germany.

With his own sense of adventure, excitement, and Oriental wisdom, SAID is perfectly suited to tell the tale of Sinbad's much-loved voyages.

RASHIN KHEIRIYEH was born in Iran in 1979 and now lives in Washington, DC. She studied graphic design at the University of Tehran. She has won many awards for her illustrations and also works for newspapers such as the *New York Times* and *Le Monde diplomatique*. Her children's books—more than fifty—have been published all over the world. In 2011 she won the Golden Apple at the Biennale of Illustration in Bratislava.

Rashin's impressive illustrations for Sinbad use a glowing palette of just a few colors. She depicts the events in her own unmistakably vivid style, and the characters always radiate a joyful, friendly warmth.

Lithography
Zieneke PrePrint
Hamburg

Design concept by
Kurt Dornig
Dornbirn, Austria

Designed by
Behrend & Buchholz
Hamburg, Germany

Typefaced in
Ingeborg by
Michael Hochleitner
Typejockeys

Paper
150 g/qm Galerie Art Vol. FSC

Cloth
Dubletta
Provided by Gebr. Schabert

Printed in Lithuania by BALTO
print, Vilnius, June 2015

Library of Congress
Cataloging-in-Publication Data
is available.

ISBN: 978-0-7358-4240-3
(trade edition)
1 3 5 7 9 • 10 8 6 4 2